I KNEW TWO
WHO SAID MOO

I KNEW TWO
WHO SAID MOO

a counting and rhyming book

written by
Judi Barrett

illustrated by
Daniel Moreton

aladdin paperbacks

New York   London   Toronto   Sydney   Singapore

First Aladdin Paperbacks edition December 2003

Text copyright © 2000 by Judi Barrett
Illustrations copyright © 2000 by Daniel Moreton

ALADDIN PAPERBACKS
An imprint of Simon & Schuster Children's Publishing Division
1230 Avenue of the Americas
New York, NY 10020

Also available in an Atheneum Books for Young Readers
hardcover edition.
Designed by Daniel Moreton and Ann Bobco
The text of this book was set in Helvetica Rounded.
The illustrations were rendered in Adobe Illustrator.

Manufactured in China
6 8 10 9 7 5

The Library of Congress has cataloged the
hardcover edition as follows:
Barrett, Judi.
I knew two who said moo : a counting and rhyming
book / written by Judi Barrett ; illustrated by Daniel Moreton.
p. cm.
Summary: Rhyming lines feature the numbers from one to ten.
ISBN 0-689-82104-2 (alk. paper) (hc)
1. Counting—Juvenile literature. 2. English language—Rhyme—
Juvenile literature. [1. Counting. 2. English language—Rhyme.]
I. Moreton, Daniel, ill. II. Title
QA113.B374 2000
513.2'11—dc21 99-31892

ISBN 978-0-689-85935-9 (Aladdin pbk.)

For one very special mom . . . mine. —j.b.

For my grandmother, whom I could always count on. —d.m.

I FOUND ONLY ONE
WEIGHING A TON
WHO HAD JUST BEGUN
LYING IN THE SUN
ON A TOASTED BUN
HAVING LOTS OF FUN
PLAYING THE ACCORDION
AND THINKING HE SHOULD RUN
BEFORE HE'S TOO WELL-DONE.

2

I KNEW TWO
WHO SAID MOO
ALL DRESSED IN BLUE
SITTING IN A SHOE
ON THE AVENUE
WITH NOSES THEY BLEW
BECAUSE OF THE FLU
GETTING A SHAMPOO
BEFORE THE BARBECUE
GIVEN BY THE KANGAROO
AND THE EWE
AT THE ZOO.
WHEW!

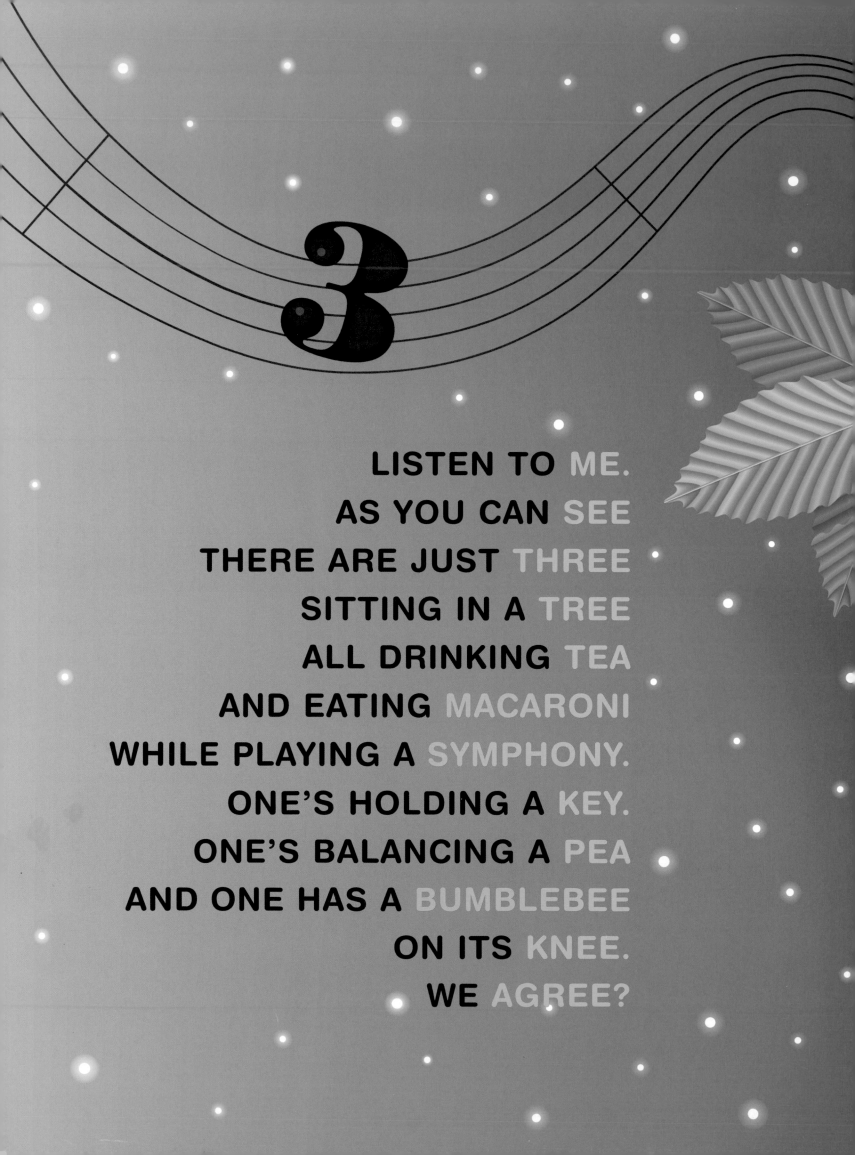

3

LISTEN TO ME.
AS YOU CAN SEE
THERE ARE JUST THREE
SITTING IN A TREE
ALL DRINKING TEA
AND EATING MACARONI
WHILE PLAYING A SYMPHONY.
ONE'S HOLDING A KEY.
ONE'S BALANCING A PEA
AND ONE HAS A BUMBLEBEE
ON ITS KNEE.
WE AGREE?

I MET FOUR
AT THE DOOR
WHEN IT STARTED TO POUR.
THEIR TOES WERE QUITE SORE
WHICH MADE THEM ALL ROAR
AND LIE DOWN ON THE FLOOR
AND WHAT'S MORE
THEY STARTED TO SNORE.

5

I WATCHED FIVE ARRIVE
AND SAW THEM DIVE
OFF THEIR HIVE
ONTO THE DRIVE.
THEY'RE ALL STILL ALIVE
AND I KNOW THEY'LL SURVIVE
AND MOST CERTAINLY THRIVE.

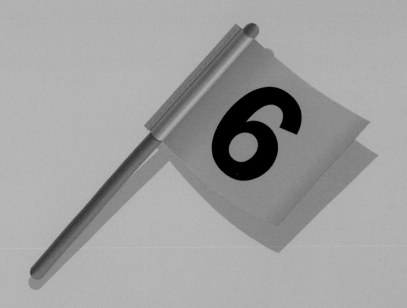

I NOTICED SIX
ALL HOLDING PICKS
TRYING TO MIX
A PILE OF BRICKS
WITH A BUNCH OF STICKS
SO THEY COULD FIX
THE HOUSE FOR THE CHICKS
WHO PERFORMED TRICKS
AND RECITED LIMERICKS.

I COUNTED JUST SEVEN
NOT ELEVEN
ALL JUMPING UP TOWARD HEAVEN.
ONE'S NAME IS EVAN.
THREE ARE NAMED KEVIN
AND THREE ARE NAMED DEVON.
"EIGHTEEN," SHOUTED EVAN,
"IS ELEVEN PLUS SEVEN."

I HEARD THAT ALL EIGHT
ARRIVED LATE
AND WERE TOLD TO WAIT
AT THE GATE.
EACH BROUGHT A PLATE
BUT BEFORE THEY ATE
THEY WANTED TO STATE
"THIS FOOD IS GREAT!"
"IT'S BEANS WE HATE."

9

I NOTICED NINE
LOOKING JUST FINE
STANDING IN LINE
IN THE SUNSHINE
HOLDING BALLS OF TWINE
POINTING TO A PORCUPINE
WITH A VALENTINE
AND A BIG SIGN
SAYING "BE MINE."

ICE CR

99¢

CHOCOLATE
VANILLA
STRAWBERRY
DIRT
SLOP POPS
MUDDY BUDDIES
HEAVENLY HOG
SWINE SWIRL
ROCKY RUNT

BE MINE
BAY OF PIGS 9
HUGGABLE HOG CHOCOLATES
PIGS SLOW CROSSING
MUD BATH
9AM–9PM
SPECIAL
Mudsicles
Señor Softee
9

THEN
I SAW TEN
WATCHING A HEN
NAMED GWEN
WRITING THE LETTER "N"
OVER AND OVER AGAIN
WITH A PEN
BORROWED FROM A WREN
NAMED BEN.